SCOPTOCRATIC

SCOPTOCRATIC
Nancy Shaw

ECW PRESS

Canadian Cataloguing in Publication Data

Shaw, Nancy, 1962–
    Scoptocratic

Poems.
ISBN 1-55022-175-2

I. Title

PS8587.H38S36   C811'.54   C93-093086-X
PR9199.3.S43S36   1992

Thanks to Jeff Derksen, Stan Douglas, Deanna Ferguson, Monika Gagnon, Lawrence Krause, Brice MacNeil, Doris McCarthy, Ken Norris, Lisa Robertson, Susanne Shaw, Colin Smith, Catriona Strang, Mina Totino, and Scott Watson.

Work from *Scoptocratic* has appeared in *Writing*, *West Coast Line*, *Avec* and *Motel*.

Cover photo: "Scene E: *The Gorge*, One may infer from this episode and begin to take an interest," by Nancy Shaw.

Published with the assistance of grants from
The Canada Council and the Ontario Arts Council.
Design and imaging by ECW Type & Art, Oakville, Ontario.
Printed by Hignell Printing Limited, Winnipeg, Manitoba.

Distributed by General Publishing Co. Limited,
30 Lesmill Road, Don Mills, Ontario M3B 2T6.

Published by ECW PRESS, 1980 Queen Street East,
Toronto, Ontario M4L 1J2.

For William Wood.

TABLE OF CONTENTS

HORSESHOE, LASSO, CUFF

There are two scenes
by no means told in conviction
the primal scene is performed
by an exalted personage.
Prior to this account:
lynx eye
without flinching
making off with it
an operation in which
no one falters.

She expresses great admiration for the landscape. Although it may be done in two or three refrains, it is by no means an end. Throwing a fur from side to side, she gives advice, explains theories, tells anecdotes, uses herself as an illustration. All this is recited in gloomy poems.

Strong conjurer
gave herself airs
showed him the terrible
the magnificent
pouring over bits of
skin and hair.

Though their relationship was closely watched, his
mind did not tend toward simplicity nor mere chron-
ology. He first took the pose in the guise of a picture
dealer. A passion prized above all by a betrayed and
ruined constitution full of cynical outbursts and invo-
cations declared by love. A case of misidentification to
which I refer the curious.

I thought I was a fly
so large, so ruffled
so intricate and oppressed.

Often winking with a
hip fitting shirt and
squirrel coloured hair
he prayed, wallowed and ceased.
So vital, so wasted
she stiffly muttered a lengthy calculation.
From that day forward her intimacy
was complete, deliciously troubled and elated.

He predicts that every aesthetic would distinguish the beautiful and the ethical, but whether he ascribes the same happiness for himself is yet to be recounted. Though this picture gives no clear impression, in my passion for its past I took to drink. I have thought of nothing else. With this certainty unmistakable as folly, I have assumed a small yet deeply disturbed following.

These are the most highly regarded:
verbal inebriation
deliciously troubled
a sadness following vivid hallucination.
About our little secret
now and then the corners of his mouth twitched
without leaving the slightest memory
as if in an indirect overture
leaving fortune, concealed vice,
vivid regrets and transports of admiration.

My letters were embellished with expressions of regret, sympathy, flattery and filial affection. There is a dutiful pleasure to this response. An eyewitness account of girlish grace. And then she became implicated by the object and recipient of his affection. Although misfortune takes the place of dreams, they are exposed to all that shrouds sticky pleasure.

This was received cordially but with indictable intentions. Marking off the lighter gestures with coarse gold links and spotted veil. Everything was disorderly, expansive and melancholy.

DEAR M:

Since our extraordinary conversation, I have thought of little else — of your studied coldness and beautiful little cigarette. I must admit to you that when the curtain rose on that dimly lit bar I listened without interest — in an atmosphere drenched with novelty and surprise. There was no evidence that this letter was actually sent to anyone. On the contrary, the deviant scenes scarcely seemed to have been mentioned. When the dishevelled man rushed in, he stood half-fashioned and politely yet fiendishly recommenced a long, eloquent, moving expression of transfigured love. He never quite regained our affection. We were left at liberty to study, criticize and admire his anticipation of a happy future.

Today I got my first compliment as a pixie. Though this does not belong in any story, we were intrigued by such a proposition. I then became associated with my series of passions for other people's lives, most of whom, by the way, I had not met. Among terms so loose, luck held over temperance, liberty and redemption. All the while the writer knew a little Latin and maintained his remarkable talent for affliction. The artist failed to take an interest in the narrator's love of telescopes. As it was her first night out as a brunette, the narrator disguised herself as a swindler, spicing her intentions with little tropes and clever puns.

The writer's clues may throw everything into confusion but he is more than a fatalist. He seeks out trios and contraptions, loafers and imposters. There is a proposition that he will leave, but only with the narrator. The artist famed for his prowess and untamed labour wanders through this over-elaborate mockery.

L.

UNREALIZED SCENARIOS

Treatment for a Film Script

The Artist is a Gambler.
The Writer a Dealer.

In a parallel description the narrator contests the course of events through her ever-auspicious reflections. Though the artist and writer move toward intimacy, emotional epiphany is surpassed by irresolvable malaise. The dealer doles out and the gambler gives away. While one is infatuated with surface, the other is with its disintegration. There are attempts to control the movement of information, but this is a function of chance. After these relations are established, they break down into difficult seduction. Throughout the narration there is a parallel tension between the impulse to accurately portray an event and the desire to embellish. All ends in rounds of admiration and self-admiration, but gestures and trivia suggest otherwise.

The narrator attenuated the dangers of her journey, investigating, establishing and hastily concluding that she could not inhabit the role of guardian or judge in search of division and paradoxes. In making this explanation she took care to moderate her voice leading to a tangle of object choices and transpositions of entire chapters. There ensue tables and equivalences that enable such an orator to express unfelt passions, a purely tactical feat with nothing so difficult in matters of love as recounting what one does not feel. Her penchant for successive reversal is notorious. As I shall attempt to show, she hired a detective to follow her then spoke of all her favourite haunts, visiting each one out of whimsical attraction. Then time ran out. Any semblance of good intentions appeared soaked in dread and speculation.

Returning to my fancy, I will continue a recital of incidental omissions. The narrator set up the library in the scene of the final encounter. This should be obvious to all — replicating the most common usage of this passage way in which until this time nothing will have occurred.

Opening Shot

Circular pan on ceiling — across the stars moving along the bar. Two men sit drinking martinis. The music stops at some heightened moment, the clink of the glasses and simultaneous sips — preparations for the opening round. Other shots can include shimmering glasses, drags of cigarettes, looks in the eye, laughter. All is anathema.

Two men speak of humiliation and loathing. She used a handkerchief to drive a jealous lover to distraction — a mere slip of the wrist. This is only too easy to believe. He broods of his own lust. The scheme is to win. All this is apprehended in a tauting manner. At first there is defiance, then punctured heat. She exclaims that this can only lead to a life in pictures. A general scheme of arousal and reconciliation. Giving formal expressions to concepts of a small flake. Apparently. Trying to avoid interpretation. In those days that was all I knew. As if there were some secret and awful pleasure.

Taking her cue from the corner of her eye she sits pensively, embellishing rancour. As if witnessing a conversation, knowing full well, listless, twinkling, justifying spyglass. This is not vanity on my part. I am quite convinced of that. He explains that a jealous lover is about to arrive. She replies suspiciously that she has seen those eyes before. Having looked at almost nothing I shall admit my foolishness to you. I returned vainly seeking.

Other Possible Descriptions

The two men begin. Without having seen each other for quite some time, they recount a problem of some intellectual propensity, of trouble to them both. With each change of scene there is a new round of drinks. Other gestures that punctuate pertinent moments include: looking in the mirror, smoking cigarettes, smoothing hair or accentuating physical features, drinking without reply, walking the periphery. Oblique, lofty reflections and speculations make little sense. One takes the position of the other, shifting from states of voyeurism, exhibitionism, narcissism and self-doubt. Cheap jokes and veiled sexual innuendo. Reversals and allusions. Discussion of erotic matters permeates talk of work — what passes between slips. All lines are rehearsed, wooden, vaguely sentimental, full of melancholy and self-regret. The strategy of faking it cuts both ways.

As I have previously stated, I'm struck by your conception. Foreseen in something despicable of less-significant spots, some private spot, some inverted vein. Heavy asphalt and lizard ring. Amber varnish and desolate red. Western and hard boiled. Needless to say, in pursuit of crime. On the mezzanine there were two rooms for looking with fine views of the ferry boat — including lyrical port scenes.

A comparison of pieces well known.
Themes of dalliance and intrigue.
All the time the words are anticipated.
I told you simply and without pride,
more simply than if I were speaking to myself.
It seemed as if others were moved
and this moved me.
I knew her very little and
that drove me to this likeness.
If I did not love, at least
I did not love some other
having looked at almost nothing
but books and ruins.
An obligatory emotion
immediately following more genuine grief.
Replacing love with cool gadgetry.

A corridor formed to replace a standard door frame.
The oval drawing room.
Along the central window frame.
The door leading beyond the corridor.

In the months permitting scandalous incursions. This reaches a pitch where nothing else is accepted as serious. Only grotesque aspects of the event dominate the circumstance.

The situation begins with a joke. A romantic, passion-ate, violent burst. A woman is placed behind the door. A third character reads as if the duration of the event is appropriate. The stranger, the husband, the gambler — nothing is known about their lives. The narrator seems sure of this. Beheld in an affecting scene. Card players in a hotel salon late at night. He has built a listening room, halls of illusion, rooms for torture. There are many theoretical fantasies.

Shooting Script

chairs and armchairs — slightly turned
an icy chateau
a frozen park
fake torches
a dull roar

Character Analysis

Turns away
toward a love seat
no doubt idle
when offered a past
a future and freedom
breaking posture
incipient tearjerker
poker chips
In the shooting gallery
felt her heart catch fire

In principle, method, order and observation lead to an autobiographical tale. To this, the role of an observer is central. The scenario can be described in detail, but most important is the placement of matchsticks on a table. By reading the intricacies of this setting, an infinite number of possibilities arise, allowing the observer or patient to decipher the outcome of events in relation to his or her disposition. It is likened to squaring off.

While one of the players has opted for luck, he speaks only of an elaboration of plans. Certain details become more valuable than others. More precisely, we are left to wonder.

I sat recounting the number of times it took him to discover the right combination. This allowed for letters, promises and libertine accounts. Fortunately, I have witnessed these symptoms before.

She repeated her famous pact in a supposedly courtly vocabulary. It is the story of three inseparables. The two lovers kissed, and I in turn was kissed by both. This was complete with all the symbolic attributes: decrees, devices, digressions and obligatory interweaving. There are suites, little houses, boudoirs and isolated estates. I have even learned of matters I did not care to know. After viewing a plethora of wilderness, I was oblivious to all but the most indignant. I failed to mention the pattern to their past while speaking in such abstractions. I have trained myself to see what others have overlooked, as I shall attempt to show by reading aloud a letter from a little-known acquaintance. Summarily, the seducer steals away, is used and returns. Normally I would find this amusing if not in sinful taste. He displayed a most impish attitude, engaged in the following manias: quibbles, haughty quarrels, riddles full of slips, denials and arguments of bad faith. There are as many entanglements as ingenuity permits, preparing the groundwork for erroneous assumptions.

The three deny that this is a quest for pleasure, as there are numerous attempts to deflect excesses of sensation and lack of distinction. There is a naive use of strategies proper to the creation of victims and dupes. To be certain, the lover is a hoarder. He was consumed and abandoned, postponing indefinitely the renewal of their liaison. Engaging in matches of pride and honour. Throwing tribute to herself.

With all my heroes off my hands, there are shifts in time
and swarms of allusions, the last of which went as such:

> Saints and sinners
> don't work out once
> the saint figures out
> she can't save the sinner.

Thus she abandons attempts at verisimilitude disguised
as erotic acts dissolving doubtful reference into furni-
ture and games. What became obvious after observing
luxurious entertainments was that the relationship
they had with others took the place of their own. To
make a comparable claim, the patient is rarely unman-
ageable. We are informed of knowledge extorted from
his confessor. This signals the completion of her edu-
cation through reading. We return suspecting that the
artist's fear of fate is somewhat freed from desire. The
writer — a note taker and blasphemer — is a charming
favorite stricken with magnificent improbability. The
narrator's elaborations are elusive and once wise. She
was charged with having taught the king to dissimulate.
Within this trifling monograph, luck has a tendency to
run out.

A fierce champion
hurls his winnings
for the historically curious

According to the logic of curiosity
a man peeps through the crack
of a nearly closed door.
She is a foreigner,
the daughter of a condemned spy

an
esquire's
artifice

There is no gun
one wears makeup
there is no sex
they go south not north
there is no blue gel

Making what he thinks
is a well-doctored drink
he apprehends the faithless
in a series of
short pointless thrusts

A courtesan
another
a younger man
his father
a faithful follower

The narrator takes her leave
grows feverish and wild
she is briefly expectant of
caddish sentiments

stricken
copula
pillars of fire

drunken but amiable
fraudulent but a good dinner speaker

open teardrops
a comely one
less lucrative than
swings and roundabouts

The story of a day's ride
and a life's romance:
trinketry
incendiary ravisher.

In simply switching roles they became
friends and apologists.
Victory is celebrated, music is heard.
He will rely on fortune.
Before a rather lengthy farewell gambling for petty
stakes he wins repeatedly playing a nervous little hand.
The three crashing chords were a slight exaggeration.
A world of gentlemen unable to act.
A grim yet elegant figure, he finds a number of clues
including a fan — a fantastic sally in questionable taste.

The narrator confesses that her recollections are entirely superficial. To promote more reputable accounts, she engaged the artist to recall intimate situations presupposing the scenario in the bar. In following through a number of themes, it occurred to him to quickly glance at each of us. He spoke of a portrait he once painted of a group mocking their master based on a popular novel of the time. Many things happened rather quickly. Although there were several furious exchanges of costume, no one penetrated his disguise. Included in the scene was a wigmaker, an ageing sailor, a virtual unknown and an essayist. There's an imposter who is exceptionally light hearted and a worldly youngster who made quite an impression on everyone. All this supposedly took place one summer evening in a quaint New York loft. When our notable host revealed himself as an amateur pianist, we learned to appreciate all that was entailed in the various murmurs regarding his misdoings. Between sittings we toured through a series of well-ordered, discretely lit rooms.

It is a pity that one cannot make a living from crafting such accounts. A glance at this text allows for further acquaintance, making industrious its entirety. In his case there was a very clever woman who spoke of a great deal during which they must have spent the night together owing to some consequence. He himself admitted that women make the best spies. Against all expectations, the argument followed suit. The man on whom she spied had recently proposed marriage to her, making an impeccable transition from one state of intoxication to another, constituting a call for some sort of sentimental suspense. She'd agreed to give him a chance. She wondered if he was a real cowboy, directing him toward a keyhole. He said he enjoyed luck, though only with strangers admitting that it would take time to get used to her new name. So the difference between the two must have occurred in the absence of any special arrangements. The third and certain conclusion is that there are no miracles. Such conclusions occur with unprecedented frequency.

They had a tremendous time making things up. The irate gardener thought it was something regarding mistaken identity. He is unfamiliar with this part of the plot, and when he realizes this, he becomes suspicious. I never fully understood the geography of that house. In it we discover who is secretly in love with the master. This episode is handled discreetly yet its impact is outrageous. Any guide or explorer is familiar. There is gradual intoxication from a skeleton in a closet — similar to engaging a bit of trickery to create a small, sensual diversion. The only possible exceptions include abandoned landscapes or scenes that require crowds. So far, nothing is new in a luminous and notorious gambling hall.

I am reminded of another configuration. These very three some years ago, met incidentally in a cold autumn chill each taking their leisure on an evening stroll. From the present vantage we are taught four relevant lessons in that very pleasant park. Passing to and fro, wrinkling per se. I recall a handsome and inviting entry and a feature patio where they were seated. On several occasions I observed such arrangements. Concurrent with this activity, some time was spent examining the movement of people in and around the park with a view to discovering who uses the area, the routes they follow and why they do so. I was reminded that there are a few singles, mostly pairs, sometimes threes and seldom more. There are more women than men. Their activity is confined to sitting quietly as they smoke and chatter. I have not observed any physical activity. My subjects, unlike those involved in such commerce, move intimately toward active entry, they are present in all weather, are touchable and totally ignored by those who walk by.

A Summary

She realized the half-finished picture formed a piquant contrast to her own. Used as a decoy in the glorious days of chivalry, she could not refrain from uttering impetuous reproaches. They had not met beforehand yet a dreaded secret lay between them. Take the victims of this disposition passionately imploding. Alarmed by outbursts, overcome by rapture they could not quell. The false friend departed grievously wounded. A beautiful singer and actress beloved by the artist whom she visited thus every day. Declaring her only interest as the subject of the present picture, which opened onto a deserted garden. Snatching the feminine garment left by the fugitive's sister. Scarcely had they gone, poured tumultuously of ill repute and brutal instincts. Not yet entirely satisfied, and seeking desperately to postpone the dreaded moment of surrender. That means we had to compel him to have no qualms. Also inflamed by his own passions to such an extent that he vowed hastily, concealing himself. He knew that she had hidden a complete set of women's clothing for his disguise. He was breathless with running and fear of recapture. She now had some means to work on his well-known jealousy. Then having possessed himself, he fell in a crumpled heap.

HAIR IN A KNOT

King and fool
hair in a
knot pins wooden
pricks I will
confess flatter my
self stop up
the mouth of.

A warm
overweening
enforce their
least they
were sin
blanket loin.

Harmless divulge
an ace in
a hole the
tripped pretty
plumb we
conceal nothing
under hats.

Hold onto
faction a
knee of a
horse sort
of specious
here for
devotion.

A prima donna's
entrance a
dictionary of
objects fame
knowledge and
fortune good
weather stops.

A tale of
villainy passion
and blood
and things
or harmless
divulge a
woman in
britches here
for devotion.

Sundered direct
suddenly applause
conspired in
favour tied
in a knot
here for
the future.

Forbidden
gloves sacred
blunder salient
tress master
the household
I'd rather
a thousand
times over
than you
you rode
the block.

Donkey skin
a fox's
tactics perched
in a tree
beak of
cheese hard
for the
more or less.

Arrived on the
porch stoop just
a little too
straight forced
him to stammer
embellished too
late.

Have you
ever encountered
flattered self
love glance
amended his
role as
banker host
decoy and
snake.

Suddenly struck
by snow
to wit.

Vain vagabond
coaxing embalm
in tones of
seduction virtue
and fortune
rise and fall
a grande
dame refuses
lavishly obscure.

An honest woman
all guilty
embellish treachery
violence and
vengeance a
habit in
short.

Scour your
body cold
disdain to
regain her
composure on
an advance
encounter a
trifling too
violent connoisseur
of fugitive
biker gothic.

Paste and ointment
bore stigmata
legitimate bride
a culpable
seduction entice
to ruin
brilliant indulgence
glut natural
wane of majesty
solemn profligate
as if every
unfull nature.

Charge suspicion
acts in
seduction
immediate ravish
glean frenzy.

Amorphous
seizure at first
glance obliged
covered his
imaginary blade
learn that
every flatterer
a thousand
times over
in a low
altered voice.

IN DOUBT A ROSE IS A GROTESQUE THING

The property line
extends to the
shore line
a dead otter
fish buoys
and driftwood.

I meant nothing by this remark.

In the interest of easing
erotic life. Fur and velvet.

In the attic
a scene of undressing
that describes the patient's life
in the language of flowers.
This was the first assertion
of her still uninhibited animosity.

With an allusion to a gift or contagion.

As you know
this is the first time
I have regretted
meeting famous personalities
miles from home.

But instead I have chosen
to investigate cadavers
perhaps a hunting scene.

Because I was reared in a hothouse
a final euphemism:
The illusion did not last.

For more than a week
failing the obvious
I was fed up with memories.

This is much more than scenery.

In a waiting room
where a picture on a wall
could spell revenge.

If I may suppose
the scene of the kiss
took place in this way.
But it was not until
the incident by the lake
that we were encouraged
and forced to make confessions.

The younger of the two was the stranger.

In a seemingly endless, paranoid view
of events, I watched from a room I
knew too well on a slender
riotous island.

With his life and mind under daily dissection.

My libidinal compliment
just as one
might refer to
inner landscape.

She'd come east in a fashion
that rather took your breath away.
Aspiring to be
the originator of moments.

There is no need for discretion.
A tremendous attraction.
An elegant adversity.

I am a natural runner.

As if a rock hit you
several times
on the head.

Familiar as it may be.

A national betrayal.
A snap of cold weather.
A hard-luck story.
Hailed with a passion.

THE ILLUSION DID NOT LAST

It began harmlessly with a question:
Who was counter-nature?

After this highly discursive introduction
another small anecdote:
at intervals of an hour
each believed herself
the true heroine.

Supposing she fell into a frenzy
somewhere between
the wish and its fulfillment.

Rumours, and rumours of rumours.
Volumes of heresy.

No longer young
as he once was
the arsonist.

Episodic testimony.

The man on whom the heavy burden
had fallen had no feeling for sights
signalling peril everywhere
in a hectic show of civility.
I thought this was typical

Later, several burning barrels of cordiality.

At least they do not notice
it in themselves
the reading of
a good life
the heroic man
bravely lashing.

Dim sheath;
that I suddenly felt this.

CINE-POEM

play my
diabolical
jigsaw

proto
renegade

violet
idler

cratic

twill

free thinkers ponder
high minded improbabilities

delectable

pimento

all very elegant

dross

looting future

panoramic hood

ungodly lick

the petty tyrant
and an unknown
third person
mention the
unslaved

supplicate
hucksters

cutaneous
aqueduct

giddy
tip

velvet	shimmy	cord
pseudo anathema	toxologic	pumphouse brocade

heap plumb
and
loin scrap

in no small part hapless

scenarist:

"what future"

I was drunk with power.

CLOSE TO NAKED

A collaboration with Gerald Creede

No movement in the sky but smoke and birds. He can't get his coat off fast enough to turn around. Dramatic rescue, insular tragedy. A slave to medic sin. Are you experts? Have you ever been experts? A soprano collapses and the opera calls a time out.

Around the next block. We always hung out in someone else's neighbourhood. Funny weather for ice cream. Raindrops on roses and whiskers on killers. Frantic tactics around midnight. Swimming in the hot sun, a mixture of bitten cork. Through a time, some play music. Cheery chords.

Figuring through the garden in a rare burst of eloquence. Someone special is waving so you must become less tearful. Next to the man with the top hat. Through the front glass. Porcelain rain.

Eliminating possibilities before they occur. They did their exercises in a public park before they were killed. This is the image being projected at home and abroad. He hallucinates breasts on silhouettes. Under eave is attic. He is to french. Just a a rolled futon is a sleep cache.

He'd had enough of intrigue. A movie night, a barbecue, a mixed dance. It had stopped wondering him. He called running the perimeter of grade school recess, 'mingling with the guests.' All the closeups are body doubles.

A touching pitch is his amplified version. Instead of going out by the side door, suddenly he clasped the girl to him and pressed a kiss upon her. From which angle and from which direction. Every house is full of things. In a second sitting, tea and biscuits on the front porch. Sketches of skyscape are never as good as the blue prints were. Delightful as it may be.

He lazed on the porch, hung like a house, spills spit and spume onto her blouse. No doubt the two of them had been seen together in the wood. Her father had then invented this fairy tale of his suicide so as to account for their rendez-vous. She tipples awhile nipple rock lull. The rival bounds through the fence in a fit rare in elegance.

She wondered an inrage of outroar. An apparent orphan. A blouse, abuse, a pose, aroused, something on paper. Kick out the raspberries. Kick out the plum. She spread her hand in the drawer and parted the red socks.

Down the next block three men stand. Looking toward us, we wait. Lips that touch service. The water's gone off. The thigh bone's connected to the cook pot. How long does it take for the next step, and please wait until the last call. His stiffened self-control rivaled all artifice. An observed luring frankness.

He was waiting until it got nicer and he could show off his shirt sleeves. Gets up, freefalls from the top bunk. Rosin from the Sandman. But the trouble had already begun, the boys spent more time in the bar than in jail. A near miss. Every time he moves his head he adjusts the balance.

71

She had been made an accomplice to the affair. Always toward the fences greener time. Often bullies on the edge of the extension, undaunted, in the sun. We were just two poor wretches who gave one another comfort. If he had a good time getting there, it didn't have to be good when he got there.

Sounds like an allegory that crowd stunned in the skyline and a hungrier child would have found out her parents were poor sooner. The older children were obedient and the younger better made, doors best left closed. Seize nature.

In another round of advice my hand awaits its forfeiture. In return objects strained. He dealt a club to his face card, losing with 23. This is something we have trouble hearing in another tradition.

From the kitchen window, the patio, the back fence. Like a diagram of the inner ear. Family scrambled. Nuptual ritual. Anal nape plan.

But what of the the unfortunate gorgeous? In the old family neighbourhood, others watch faithfully. Someone is waiting. The sugar falls from the slit in the box slow as time sand. An index to the second lines. A wise decision.

And now only numbered glances across the view. Certain to undone. Vertical is certain. Whore is optional. Usually in June, though, their daughters would marry. Film tactics. Hankies. Her father, a man of some perspicacity, guessed that the girl had no serious suicidal intentions.

Almost always we were called to the view. In the privacy of my own rent I suspect the rip in tenancy. Sperm spills, a dull lanolin squirt in a cornucopia apparition. The penis was shaped like 1/3 of Zorro's signature. His works did not always tally with his animosity. "Get in by sundown or" — or this guy clear and cloudless.

Biting off bits of cork and spitting them in the toilet bowl, buoy of spunk afloat in scum, low cal, skim. Full natal penetration. A gesture of doing.

At the corner store the older kids told us: "The lonely die alone and the loved, poor and attended." Could the kiss have taken place in this way. The gaps were to be found in her memory. Sundown and sunset. The late sun. An off-hand jerk off.

Zealous reformers in the community centre seemed to bask in the suspicion that they might be. With heels to the ground, their nakedness was a detail. The illusion of brilliance and suspense. A roll of quarters in his shorts pocket. Confronted with regimentation at the entrance of a crowded enclosure. No explanations were in order. Unreasonable melancholy . . . this brightly coloured pill.

A gift for concealing facts, with nothing so self-considered. He had covered the distance that had made his return impossible. I can see from the light shining through your rib cage that you've a fine skeleton. Out of sight, out of jail. The stigmata of sensibility. A maraschino cherry in the hot sun. Wait for September. Whore is ontological. Whore is until.

I hear lazy fans shunt imaginary air, the office laden with waiting, the exchange desultory and tropical. Autonomous. Propaganda work is now compulsory. After you're treated as a whore so long, you get casual about how you dress. She uses nail polish to gum up a run, a caustic arousal. He'd as lief take his chances in the past. Powder is reasonable and talc is cheap. They don't open it to finger, they open it to show. It can get in anything air can get in. The map of three oil spills went into effect. Lips that touch Icarus. That's why they carried rods in their top hats. If you got hepatitis you could claim to have been swimming in the river.

The delight he takes of observation, its suggestion of escape, innuendo. He enjoyed his parents' wedding pictures because he didn't know them yet and they looked like nice people. Below this quasi-subterranean stream. Alluring — a vague and modest idea of himself as a legendary frame. An inexplicable contempt, counting somewhere in the back of his mind. Usually in June, on the edge of greener time.

Concocted, encroached, circled. She wore a green dress in this socialist spring of reasonable doubt. They gathered in front of the camera, allies on the lake. The crash is a tragic part of this community. They perished together, three years into the mandate, cured to celebrate the death of two martyrs. Two of their fellow fighters.

To be embraced or sustained by the light-green, hoisted to the short portages. Uproarious reunions. Close up, close to naked, accosted arousal. You might have seen him naked, standing on the shoulder, waiting for a chance to cross. The police took his pulse as they drove by.

In exploring the circumference of an inner window he detected two moles. A no-frills operation. Dress shields in the forefront of battle. In time they'll just vanish. Body double. Voice over.

He had signed nothing, vowed nothing, pledged nothing. Full and forward. Don't pass out — put out. From the backroom window it is clear and cloudless. Then he covers the distance that makes his return impossible. The illusion of brilliance and suspense. A stab is the gesture, not the knife, or the cut. Buoyant, full afloat.

He had a fortunate childhood in that though reading was his closest comfort it wasn't his only one. To become a national obsession, complete with good guys, bad guys and fallen heroes. Enough lessons to swim out of reason. He made a tent on his lumpy bed by tucking one end of a threadbare sheet under the far end of the mattress and the other end up over the headboard letting the flannel fall away like canvas flaps, pegging it with ruined slippers between the paint-splotched wall and fractured wood under which he read (coaxing the dying bulb on a rusty flashlight), novels that nurtured middle-class emotions he didn't yet know he had no right to. In her estimation there were a lot of fine memories, a common presence. On the last day the buwley bugs skittered up the headpost. On these grounds, he could avoid damaging publicity. Interrogated, but not held in violation. Paving every kilo of secondary road. The wish built into the library.

On the cornerstone of the community centre, while the cement was still wet, some kid had written Fuck God and drew a heart around it. He just said he heard it, he didn't say he believed it. He used the cup she used a few days before finally washing it. While the cement was still yet. And another drink without courage. He wants to make certain, (he wants to kill a little time).

He once whaled in the arctic. I was in my room, it wasn't me. There is only one logical answer. A commitment to detail. Shining face, stunning force. A flat form for everything. You can't afford the luxury of previous experience. The imposter may be identified by the scratches on his face. I've lost my will apparently in double.

Refrain:

ON MY RETURN FROM A FAR FETCHED FIELD

A man pushing his woe on the way to a thrill. Broke. What happened? He fixed a target to a convenient tree, in theory, at any rate. At the end of her domain reached by a small circular staircase a prepossesing woman, though, she ceased to be his mistress. All puffed up, a real little lift.

Nevertheless, she gave it her name
the mad science of a bee's pollen
a habit of calling it hers.

IT'S ALWAYS THE GOOD SWIMMER WHO DROWNS

The only complete stationary object in the room. Their hands, set lightly, never quite chatter. If she saw me out of the corner of her eye, she gave no hint. As you may imagine in the course of this adventure. About her life as a *femme fatale*:

Good mother.   Devoted father.
So obliging.   So amusing.

Unforgettable days.

In principle, always answer yes. In this instance, the relation of confusion and the patient's life. Hence, it was for years that she kept the portrait of herself. *The horse was as good as the rider.* A submitting display. A place at every table, at the next table. That all goods be held in common.

The two details of their behaviour:
A speedy marriage.
To arouse natural instincts.
The latter is never attempted. The former only tried,
owing to motives that will only later become evident.
Scenes of married life. Horseback riding. Rain bistro. A
traditional grouse shoot. After much study, the eternal
victim.

I shall spare myself the details, but by the beginning of the last chapter, the hero's horse rarely wins. He admitted the scene had probably occurred one or two years later. Without having heard myself, I explain this by supposing I spoke to them out loud. In a way *that* was not at all remarkable.

Of that celebrated affair:

Spectacle.	Romance.
Action.	History.

Ravaged hearts. Squandered fortunes. An unauthentic revolution. Back to his early life. A change of scene. Happy days despite the weather. I have seen your portrait.

You will observe a set of pitiful misadventures and accidents. An ordinary object or scene. A sudden flare. The said clock, wound up. On the dangers of curiosity. Figurative pity. Ill-considered intimacy. A calculated plan for doing good.

Only fear of seeming so. I shall finish as I began with a timely and well executed attack. I am a man of the circus. Mere examples: to put one in the picture. Stand still. Shadow show. The most wonderful, fantastic episode: If, I . . . Nevertheless, he was not at all a scandal machine. That it should come to this.

The elements of the tenth year, described by the hero in the first hour, are not merely as he supposed. Tyrants have other means of seduction. Then she told the story for the third time. In the shape of a vow. A recital of debts, in pantomime, with tableaux, and acrobats.

One false move.
                    Rumour. Scandal. Passion.

That he became her bodyguard. I have watched you
discreetly. One may infer from this episode and begin
to take an interest in nature. Ascertaining all her habits.
And so on. That the father met the daughter in the
company of a lady.

The very element of seduction. These few words should have been enough. The temperament of this situation might have seemed intriguing. And so on. Triumph and perdition. The twelve elements of an ideal life to which we were sworn. The displacement with which they had become involved in reproducing these details.

A certain natural duplicity extended to this end, completely motionless. You might have found it amusing. I turned my consideration to our safety. In perfect view, only a stupid question. The history of surrender in greater detail. All that had passed or rather she appeared to have been saying.

I will only add at the end:

Complete. Character. Obsession.

Happened to fall to his feet. Names that were of little consequence. And immediately, in accordance with a type of procedure with which she was familiar. According to the wording, we were obviously very fond of cruelty.

The first part, with questions: a charming inn, a good dinner. The most indelicate. The most indecent. At the time perhaps, he hesitated. If one may use such a phrase. A case of prudence or impending arrival. It could have happened fifteen years ago.

DEAR M:

In this swiftly moving, scintillating masterpiece I realize it is difficult to remember that it is intended to be thoroughly revolutionary. I was logically constrained by the subject at hand, but those who know me are sufficiently curious to lend indulgence. I feel unburdened that the episodes were occasioned by longing, and I shall be grateful for memories of those times considered to be indispensable to such elucidations.

And I thank you for engaging in such intimacies ripe with habit and repetition, detail and excess. My fictitious gems are often abandoned in favour of the previously unseen. Though I warn you of the risk and inertia accorded to the observer eccentric to accumulation and serendipity. Under your ever watchful eye, I present this to you as a series of small adorable gifts.

There is no reason to respond to each of my trifling jokes, because at present I have habitually written to you but have avoided to confide that I no longer believe in detective fiction. These recollections were puzzling though gifted and clever. If this is nonsense, I cannot tell. The tone seems obvious, but if it were improved it may present further difficulties in the strangest guise — perhaps no more than a tickling sensation in the back of the neck. If I fail to convey to you any ideal of the quiz master's finesse, nothing is new or so you seem to suggest.

I have told you everything that is possible and I come to say farewell. The gardener is too coldly written in seeing him for what he might become. I urge you to try your luck.

You accuse me of faulty conclusions. I reply with tender misanthropy resuming an unpredictable course. I was absorbed in the usual fantasies on the heels of keen pleasure. I am self-seeking, and certain details should not be mentioned. We have no need of doing so, this story is very clever.

Suffice it to say that I am no investigator — recalling written scenes by the lake thusly enacted. A final bond or notice of elaboration is as superfluous as other promises. I fail to understand your attraction to gambling halls. As if this twisty speech proves key.

I continue to work vigorously and in solitude. You are still owed details and I send you a solution: there are almost always compromises and formulations as surplus precedes transfiguration. Some say he's a naked and bleeding heart. I become whimsical, glued to my seat, full of simple retort. Involved in this volume is the release of unpleasure unavoidably glossed over.

Write often, my old friend, and tell me again and again that we may not be compelled. Further to this I have nothing to tell you. What you have to say, I already know. In a realization of an old wish, you may look and say that you hoped to be involved, but appreciation is radically diminished by a temperature causing us to craze. I recall driving toward the horizon, toward a wise and blissfully reminiscent view full of familiar rhymes, stolen words and pithy phrases. According to this trifling logic, promiscuity only creates the illusion of distance. A slight twinge remains to be seen.

Lurking behind ever-popular belief is my heartfelt thanks and an explanation you will no doubt cast away. Although appearing clumsy, accept my thanks, admiration and warmest congratulations for allowing this to be fashioned after all your very elegant, long, intense, informative letters.

L.